RENEE C

Juice

KELSEY ST. PRESS

Grateful acknowledgment is made to the editors of *Fourteen Hills,
Gare du Nord,* and *How(2)* where earlier versions of *No Through Street,
Proportion Surviving,* and *First Sleep* appeared.

Special thanks to Rachel Bernstein, Aja Duncan, and Jen Hofer
for their close readings of this manuscript.

Copyright © 2000 Renee Gladman

Library of Congress Cataloging-in-Publication Data
Gladman, Renee.
   Juice/Renee Gladman.
     p. cm.
   Contents: Translation – Proportion surviving – No through street – First sleep.
   ISBN 0-932716-55-5
   I. Title.

PS3557.L2916 J85 2000
813'.54—dc21

                                              00-064655

Cover illustration: Andrea Nelson
Cover and interior design: Lory Poulson
Printed by McNaughton & Gunn

The text is set in Optima.

Kelsey St. Press 50 Northgate Ave, Berkeley, California 94708
                    phone 510-845-2260   fax 510-548-9185
                    email: kelseyst@sirius.com
                    web site: www.kelseyst.com

Distributed by: Small Press Distribution   800-869-7553
                  email: orders@spdbooks.org

**NATIONAL
ENDOWMENT** Publication of this book was made possible by grants from the
FOR THE ARTS National Endowment for the Arts and the California Arts Council.

Contents

TRANSLATION

7

PROPORTION SURVIVING

21

NO THROUGH STREET

29

FIRST SLEEP

47

for Chubby

> In the modern narrative, time seems to be cut off from its temporality. It no longer passes. It no longer completes anything.
>
> — Alain Robbe-Grillet

Translation

About the body I know very little, though I am steadily trying to improve myself, in the way animals improve themselves by licking. I have always wanted to be sharp and clean. But this is not a story about me. This is about those of us who live among the great ink-stained mountains, the ones between the Twelve Cities and that little island. It is a simple tale, not too much to worry about. Though I have cut corners to get here, these are the basics of my story: the fact of everybody's disappearance, a conviction of flight and return, and a loneliness so startling that people will want to paint it.

Everything I know began the first summer I was in an archeological gang. The leader, undeniably a subject of consideration, was my mother's lover. It was a dynamic time between them as well as between other lovers in our town. Let me tell you about this town. Most people will say they have not heard of my town; even those with imagination will deny it. But you will never see a more spectacular place. From our General Store to our smallest rocks, we have something. It's not class — I can only compare it to stature. We have statues that the sky illuminates to such a degree that we live in them. They aren't mirrors; they are magnificent distractions of great height and fortitude. They are brick and handsome.

When I describe these mountains, people think they must be in the south. That's reasonable. Or maybe it's the way I talk about them that's southern. As children, we were trained to speak peripherally about ourselves. Teachers directed our attention to our surroundings though never detailed them. We were to mature by impression alone. I have been shaped by this region's perplexing history. You see, the people in this town migrated from the island off the "declining" coast — that is how we have endeared it, our old declension and sinking feeling — in escape of too much tyranny and discriminating stuff. My relatives, attracted to facial markers, saw these now familiar stains and settled here. It was unequivocally empty — another thing ground into us — we were nobody's conqueror.

The town established a gang of archeologists to explore the facts of our extended history. It seems that some relatives were in a hurry and gave abbreviated narratives. They dropped bottles as they climbed mountains — bottles now holding the key to vitals. The town took a child from every family, plus each child's third eldest cousin, and started to call us a gang. We were to recover items from a long list of missing things. As I have said, it was a great time to be in the mountains. Communication between lovers was spatial, so many things to wrap oneself around that actual contact was not desired; one was satisfied with what seemed like endless possibility, and so, dwelled in that. I have grown to find that I need only to think of people for physical pleasure. I think it's these mountains, their looming presence, that make feeling beyond the mind too strong.

I love this town. It's still vibrant though I have not seen anyone in years. I am not in jail — they just have gone. I cannot remember where I was when I came back to find them gone — maybe at the river or drying my hair in the hot part of the forest. All I know is the sudden ghostliness of it. Imagine having loved something for so many years that you don't see it anymore. I mean, you feel it, but so synonymously with the flow of your blood or taking in air that the beauty seems to be about you. Life was that dynamic. We could not love ourselves more. Well, imagine coming home to a one-hundred-mile expanse of beauty that you always have thought of as yourself, and finding on that day that it exists without you. Furthermore, contemplate the disturbance of that compounded by the apparent exodus of those who, in your mind, were extensions of yourself.

The emotion behind this story is colored by events that would be lethal to repeat. That is, their unfolding would unleash a polluted something beyond anyone's comprehension. No science can explain what propels this story. The land can hardly contain its volatile nature. Anyone observing my predicament would wonder why I have continued on. But, in a way, because there are no observers, I have no choice but to go on.

I am the youngest of eight very mild-mannered kids. My oldest brother was a pioneer. That is, he discovered a place that was not too close to our present lives where we could store our heirlooms. The town as a whole felt discomfort around these "gifts" from the past, as on a ship passengers tend to avoid the anchor. In order to believe in them, we did not want to see them. One day, my brother stumbled upon an annex — really a break in the mountain or narrow upper cave — and a mustiness made him venture inside.

First the town thought it could be City Hall, but there was not enough room for chairs. It took some time to realize its use, years to uncover our suppressed untidiness with regard to our totems. We could not face the proximity of the past and did not want to use it either. People slowly began to bring my brother their worn-out things, which their forefathers had left them. He stored them in the slit of that mountain, teasing the town about its "past shelter." And that is how we came to know it.

My new home is right outside the shelter. Of course I would want to go there and hang out with the things that root my people. The hope being that upon their return I will have missed them less. If it seems like I'm all right, then my own experiences elude me. I have demonstrated a series of symptoms ranging from tiredness to eyestrain. I am mostly defenseless and, the most difficult thing of all, forced to reacquaint myself with the characteristics of this land — the wind, drastic temperatures, loneliness, seductive beauty and roaming shade of the mountains — with the same mind, but a very different heart. This morning, I made myself climb a tree. I had not eaten in eight days, having stood beneath that tree, coveting its fruits and leaves, but without the strength to scale it. Last month, there were voices in my dream. Voices direct and full of passion sounding strange in my dream. I think they were my ancestors. I mean, I think that's where hope comes from.

When I manage to eat I have the whole town in mind. Eight months ago, I came upon a school of fish. What I felt in my mind symbolized one of two things, each thing having something crucial to do with the town. I ate fish after fish, hoping that I was feeding something in me, or that what I wanted to be in me — the people of this town — would suddenly appear before me.

I am not concerned about how the townspeople will express themselves upon their return; they could come in happiness or in extreme anger and it would not bother me. The point is that they return.

There are games one plays while one is waiting for a mass return; they are mostly sexual. I cannot help but be sexual before these mountains, their flirtish behavior and exquisite face. I find that I am moved to ecstasy — ecstasy being my most treasured activity. I would rather have the town, but will miss the nakedness of these years.

But regarding what I was saying about self-improvement — it is a hard thing to prove. You can't just walk up to someone, or in my case a plant, and say, "Hey, look at how I've grown." You have to wait for the person to notice. This morning I thought the Crassula noticed, but I can't be sure. Every day what I've learned about the world recedes a bit — I can only guess at what we were. I know that I am not the "me" of ten days ago — I certainly don't look like that "me" or how I thought of her.

As a product of this region, change within the body is easy. In winter, we put on pounds to survive, shedding some of them in the summer. I always wanted to be a little heavier each time around. The town grew nut trees to supply our fatty foods. There would always be a crunching sound to remind you of your seasons. In the fall, people crunched from the first sign of morning through five o'clock in the evening. In spring they crunched only in the evening. Summer feeding, limited to a two-hour crunch, was my favorite season. But now I cannot bring myself to hold a nut let alone plant it. And if my mom knew — she will know as soon as she returns, the whole town will know. They'll scream at me about their nuts, saying, "Where are the nuts? It is cold. Where are the nuts?" Of course that is me assuming that it will be winter when they return. These days it is me assuming everything. I don't know how long I will last. My moods, these mountain moods . . . yesterday I tried to climb the central mountain and it would not yield, for hours my right foot slipping. But each time, as I grew near the brink of madness, a breeze sauntered through me. It was the temperate climate of this region, ruining then saving me. Every day there is a different element to save me. I would have given up long ago if it were not for . . . and so on. You get to a point in isolation where you have to grab the reins; you can't let the silence get to you. Survival with the town was congenial. Without them, it is processy.

When we came together as a town to fight the various plagues, it was the intense regularity of our meetings that kept us involved, fortifying the strength known as the town's children. As a child I was assigned to gather things to help us with our flus. My brother, as I have said, handled the spatial things. The Brinkley kids, though lazy, farmed the meat things. We were coordinated in a tribal way.

Many years back there was a virus ravaging us — made the black skin of my neighbors turn toward the moon. At the time, I was too young to be affected by the cycles of the moon. Bear in mind, this is a land without normal science. The Floyds' oldest boy was the only one to decipher that science, but he was sick. I'm trying to tell you how I knew we were a tribe. It was not by the length of our feet or color of skin on the inner sides of our hands that I knew it. We were tribal in our language, in the way ideas came to us. Approaching us as we would a Saturday afternoon visit, coming to each of us — for a moment until we were almost full, then leaving us a little lonely. The ideas brought us out into the street, backs to the mountains to face the little island — First Island. A different group chosen for every disaster, *seeing* that island and finding words for the ideas. A good direction that is a composite of a few communal lives. This time I was the townsperson in the middle of the street, not fearing the voices that spoke to me. I knew what I had to do. At least a part of what I had to do; the woman standing next to me knew the rest. Or just enough to have what the man knew next to her close it all up. We headed out, as a tribe would head out, in search of our remedy.

When a tribe has been reduced to one, there is no talk of remedy. Well, there is no talk. As a town, we had the most intriguing conversations. Now I play with leaves.

So far it has been sex and leaves that keep me alive.

———

I think it was two years ago that the first visions appeared. Magnificent figures fluctuating between a dark gray and a darker one. They were astounding in their depth and dullness. Anything brighter would have been too much for me.

There are certain things about the spirits I figured out. For instance, they knew me — a few moments into their initial visit I could tell they had thoroughly studied me. Well, I thought that would mean something — communication might be clearer or anything except what it did mean. You see, these figures had no voices. My town had gone and the only semblance of humans that I'd since seen were not humans at all, but photolytic patients who were lonelier than me.

For the first year I saw them every day. They were funny spirits; they liked to stand around and pantomime, intending to provoke me. But the problem with gesturing spirits is that their natures are too serious. One does not believe them. The spirits knew that they could not inspire me. But, once they knew they could not inspire me, we were able to move beyond that point. It did not take long to see what we had in common, the most important thing being time.

Spirits are said to teach people about death. When they come and there is nobody dead, then they themselves want to be taught. I taught the spirits two things. But that does not matter. What matters is now they are gone as are the voices in my head. It also seems that the Brillow bird is gone — two native plants and the seed moth are gone. The mountains are not gone. My energy is gone, but my love for the townspeople is not. We are disappearing from lack of diverse biologic systems. No real cell mutations to think on.

To save this land I have to bring back archeology. As a child this thought was implanted in me: In the appearance of any species there is an element of its disappearance and within its disappearance a particle of return. And that is why we have storage. My brother told me this. It's good that he told *me* since I am the only one near the past shelter.

In our past there is a germ for survival, beneath our weathered clothes and yellowed papers, a propellant of time. If I wanted to I could spend the rest of my days devoted to time. Or end the township here for something on the other side of the mountains . . . is there life there? Well, it does not matter if there is life because I am not leaving this mountainside. It has been six years since the exodus. A year since I last spoke. I have forty-two years left of health, and anticipate five hundred years before the great tidal wave. Things here slowly returning to slime and translation.

Proportion Surviving

Long before the fresh apple crisis, my life had some form to it. I would wake in the mornings—I would perform something. For example, the day I tried, as one with acute passion might, to win one woman over but accidentally won another—that whole time I had been living like someone. Though I can't remember his name. His model of optimism provided me with a certain geography that I inhabit in time of need. This time the need was surprising. People tend to have faith that the juice they drink in the morning is the same juice they have always drunk. And apples take their shape naturally. The guy, whose name escapes me now, taught me to look upon others' concerns as mine to make at home. I was fond of doing many things at home, but my favorite was drinking juice. When my friends came by—they liked to suddenly show up with all kinds of breads in their hands, thinking they knew what I needed and planning to force it on me—I had to tell them I was busy with my juice. Two weeks before the crisis, I had been writing some poems about it. It was a warm day, not entirely different from other warm days in San Francisco. People were on the street. Pale people were on the street, making it to the park and lying there such that the next day they were a little browned. The poems I had written were failures, but dense ones. It seemed appropriate to think the person's attempt at wholeness was a series of missteps, which if drawn across an afternoon might prove interesting to other people. I had a way of reminding my friends that we were all in pain, but a fruit tart kind of pain strangers can't help but enjoy. That day I had, in a sense, gathered all my possessions and gone out onto the street with them. I awoke that morning with an urgency to prepare myself for something—not anything life threatening, but definitely personal.

My lover, then, wanted to spend much of her life asleep. She had no ostensible reaction to the city's sudden depletion of all its fresh apples and no hope for them. In a world where a person's tastes revolve around the kind of sleep she gets, I could not find four people who cared. I thought that if I could find those four people we could really do something. A few of my friends pretended they were chosen. A few neighbors felt bad and made offers. My mother called to console me. My lover—in actuality, the closest person to being a member of the encumbered troop, slept next to me. Sleep became our network: falling in and out of it for change. The rule of survival is that no two people can lie in the same bed and sleep at the same time. So I kept an eye on her and played this game of freshness. If by morning I could quickly run out and do seven things that did not involve longing, she would reward me. Before the crisis, the reward would have needed only to be an apple one. But after the apples were gone. The landscape usually contains the solution to what's lost. Demographics help people in cars. Some people did not notice me. Some demographers lose sleep and do not notice me. That was two days before. The evening before it was two days before the crisis, I was thinking that I did not think I was asleep. I had been watching the sunlight take the corner of my room and my housemate's cat in it. When I looked again, there was no light—but I had not been asleep. It's the way people react to traumatic events. They say, "I had just been there" or will say, "She was just with me." So the loss of light was emotional and the lost state—demographic. I began to trace things by their disappearance. Alone in the room, my memory, and anticipated darkness going for light. People like to talk about the daytime. People in strange moods often miss the daytime. Before the crisis it was not often that one would find me in strange moods. I had managed a particular kind of balance fortified by a certain satisfaction of taste. I was happy. I mean, I was in my juice.

Five weeks before the crisis, I was employed at the natural foods grocery around the corner from my house. I did not really work there, but I went there every week. All but the third Sunday of each month, I would walk in and find all kinds of juice on sale. Not to buy, but to stand next to. Shorter people have the privilege of proximity to most cardboard signs. That was the thing. I would stand there and be something for taller people who couldn't see. I had gotten into the habit of improvised customer service as a way to peruse the juice aisles without being noticed. My parents thought my talents should have led me somewhere. My father would always say, "If you're not going to be a people person, then numbers will have to do." He was surprised that with all the time I had on my hands, I chose to spend most of it alone. Numbers then did hold some mystery for me, but mostly too high and far-reaching to explore. For years I had known that if there was a wall between where I was and where I needed to be, I did not want it there. Some people have personal goals that are demanding. Certain goals make it impossible to lounge around in bed. My decision to drink only fresh juice, which costs as much as a small satisfying breakfast, kept me busy rounding up cash. I would have to leave most friendships behind. As a way of keeping my life "wall-free," I had to divide my time. I would spend the first part of the day searching for volunteer positions in organic juice factories. The second part of my day I would spend telling people about the first part. The other parts are not of substance here.

Twenty-five years before the crisis I had for the first time what would eventually become known to me as apple juice. Twenty-three years later a magazine editor would reject my first attempt to recount that experience in litany. I am always drinking in my poems, a good friend says.

In the first years of my life, everything I ate was mush. Today I will tolerate only the toughest of green vegetables and date people who will always forget this. When I had that remarkable glass of apple juice, I had no idea that one day I simply would not be able to find it. The city gets rid of its apples. People find themselves inventing fruit. The day I decided to write poems about it—it was twelve days before the rumors began and fourteen days before the media coverage—I had been resting in my best friend's easy chair. We were discussing the rise of the smoothie industry when something fantastic occurred to me. Five days later I had twenty poems. When a person writes a poem about her passions, people on the street are bound to notice them. The passions overwhelm the body. She carries the body as though it were the book. The friend whose easy chair gave way to my failures moved out of town the next week, and though I miss her it was the failures that saved me. On every other day of any kind of crisis one finds particular sayings helpful. If certain words are spoken quietly into a cup of hot water, with the handle of the cup turned towards the wall, whatever strength found in the person may be mirrored in the wall. The person leaves the house with her hand against this wall but strutting slightly.

In the alley behind the natural foods grocery, I met my second lover for the first time. Meeting people in vulnerable places accentuates the passion later. Or it may be so hot that the lover never thinks in the present. And the weather was so hot during the crisis. Only the alleys had shade. Forty-eight days into the crisis, while on a thirst strike, I had to make a run for the alley. Not as though people were after me, but the elements. The foundation of anyone feeling that they must get away is need; at the bottom of any body-based need is grace. When I appeared at the opening of the alley, a woman who not twenty-four hours later would be dozing in my bed was stacking crates against the east-side wall. Women who work against surfaces inspire me to things—I thought about telling her, or—short women make me want things. All the time while I was growing up I put a lot of demands on my juice; forty-eight days into the crisis she made me forget it. I did not forget it, but was embroiled. The newspapers were saying things about the past. People were celebrating thick juice, and I kept writing those poems. That day in the alley I realized three things about life. While assisting her I learned three things to carry around with me, to disperse when needed. For six months during the crisis, I did not care about the crisis.

When my faith returned all my lovers were gone. That morning I woke to the two hundred and thirty-second day of the crisis; I was beneath my bed. It was the sixth day that I had awakened beneath my bed. I was lonely, but I was also sure. Life without juice had taken on the name and shape of my weakest character, who—when we passed on the street—did not know me. I knew it was me by the way my head felt: people find themselves in an idea and feel so specified by the idea that they are compelled to show it. Today all my ideas are liquid. That day of my faith, friends thinking I was sick came by to see me. It would be the last day I spent alone; I was happy, but still would not drink. The juice on my mind was no longer juice. There was an absence there, but one so constant it became familiar. I did not want to drink it.

No Through Street

On the first day of my return to Hershey Street, I convinced myself that the buildings before me were not buildings but eager placards suspended in air. For them to be buildings, I would have to say that the houses that used to be there were gone and I could not say that. Instead, I paid a lot of attention to the names, observing their buoyancy: Golson & Bros., without a body. Crispy Crème Cuisine. I counted thirteen names on the not-buildings and felt sad about the emptiness.

—

Fifteen years ago, as I walked along the tree-lined street toward my now-past future, I saw Mr. Godfrey standing on the edge of his lawn in utter fascination of something. When I think about it, I am sure that he had witnessed the chaos that I am now seeing. What else could explain his suddenly heaving chest and the way his eyes glazed over when they turned to me?

I remember the thing he was looking at—the thing that sparked the vision. It was a directional painted by my sister. It read "No Through Street." She had painted dozens of signs for Hershey Street by the time she was fifteen. The signs told people which way to go. Everyone thought *No Through Street* was brilliant. They had never seen anything like it, never anything written that made so much sense. Before she painted that sign, Hershey was considered only an alley. Now it was a "No Through Street."

When I left home it was not with the hope of arriving any place. I had gone out to look and never came back.

"Looking" is an activity moving on the conviction that there is more to seeing than sight; my sister introduced the possibility to me. There was a wooden fence surrounding our house that creaked through the night. She wanted me to go look at it. The night was mild, so I wasn't worried about the cold. The sky was clear. If there had been anything she needed to show me in the sky, that night I would have been able to see it. But my sister said looking had nothing to do with the sky.

The first hour we listened for the creaks; in the second we tried to find them. It is true that wood creaks. She was not trying to fool me in that. But I did not know that I couldn't find where it creaked. That night I traced my hand along the weathered contours of the fence. I got splinters. I found the smooth spots that were hard to move away from. I had fantasies. I looked that night as a ten-year-old would. The next time I looked, a few weeks later, I was twelve.

On another night: Two small girls stand on top of one hundred pounds of dirt at a construction site. It is near eleven o'clock. They stand, on the night of the new moon, in a frightening darkness. The older one sings while the younger one looks.

I saw us in the fifteen-foot-high glass leaning against a half-built concrete wall. I don't remember what they were building, and now I'm not sure if it was really glass. But our reflections, in that cavernous night, were illogically—in my young mind—thrown back at us. My sister instructed me to see how we could be there even though it was so dark. I aged after that looking. Every occasion on which I looked, I was inevitably aging.

One day I outgrew everything there was to see.

Six days after my return, I stood again at the head of Hershey Street, still unable to surrender my past to its obvious transformation. It was by accident that I found myself there. An attractive woman on Mueller and Third had given me a smile of recognition and then taken off fervently toward Hershey. I followed her because she was the first person I had seen in a week who knew me. I followed her because she was extremely tall, and no matter how far ahead she jogged, it was impossible to lose sight of her.

After five minutes or so, I hit what felt like a wall. I looked up and saw the sign *Hershey St.,* and found that I could go no farther. Because the woman had forgotten me or did not notice that she remembered me, she kept going. I was frozen on the corner. I'm sure there were people around who could not help but stare at me. But there was nothing I could do. Ten beautiful people could have walked enthusiastically down my former street, smiling and waving at me, and I would not have been able to move a step closer.

———

Between the moment fifteen years ago when I turned the corner away from Hershey Street and a year later when I "woke up" outside a Midwestern hotel, there is water where memory should be. There was evidence in my bags, my pockets, that made me think I had been on trains. There was the way I kept looking over my shoulder—back east—that reminded me of trains. So that's where I assumed I had been, and that is where I went.

I have spent my life on the passenger trains going east to west. It is possible to experience love on the trains. I learned that, and also that it is possible to be surrounded by death on the trains.

On passenger trains most windows are good for viewing, but for looking things go by too fast. I had to give it up—it was hard. Then I learned some things. Besides love and death, I began to acquaint myself with the human voice. On trains you hear more than you see—of the train. I spent eight years slouched in my seat so that I could not see. People on trains are intent on arrival. If you look at them, I believe they could become paranoid. A person, about to arrive, could start yelling that you were following her. Because I lived on the trains, I did not want to be associated with that kind of embarrassment. So, those I could not love and who did not throw themselves from the trains, I slouched and listened to.

When the trains neared a destination, some women's voices got low. Kids stopped crying. Apart from the presence of voices, there were also the unavoidable reminders of the body. I grew up hearing the sound of men's bones crack as they stood against the swoosh of younger men's organs. These were the sounds of the traveler. The porters and I carried our bodies in silence.

For twelve of the fourteen years that I know I was on trains, I was wondering about my body.

For the last three of the fourteen years, I had vivid dreams of my long-lost street.

———

A painter's horizon may simply be the designation of such, the ability to state which way to go. She can grow up and want only to paint, but the paint does not have to extend beyond that point. It could show itself as a street sign.

A public craze brought the media to Hershey Street. Of the hundreds of signs my sister painted, it was the late '80s series that brought the crowds. The signs shed a new light on decision making. When one approached them—for instance, in the middle of the night—one sat struck by the depth in them. But not for long. The signs were not designed to stall people.

When the journalists saw my sister's work they wrote about it with zest. This sparked critical attention and, later, the consuming crowds. Six months into her nationwide acclaim—I would later discover—the first of my long-time neighbors, the Godfreys, moved out. They left behind them an emptiness that caused panic in those remaining. But I don't know much more than that.

I do know that fame comes ravenously to a place that is not prepared for it, and though it does not mean to eat the place, it does.

When the media and museum-goers had consumed the last of our street, I was waiting between trains in Philadelphia. My hands shook as I read about it in the newspapers. I was in misery, and also it seemed that the train would never come. When it finally came I had no drive to return to Hershey Street. For the next few days I walked in and out of Philadelphia's Union Street station, unable to board a train leaving in any direction.

My sister lives in the warehouse district on Southeast Bellmont. There is a sign outside her building that reads "Just Outside Bellmont." I am almost certain that she painted it, but not positive, because I have not seen her to ask. I have been walking around the city making guesses about her—wondering which signs are hers and which ones belong to her followers.

Yesterday morning I stood for an hour in front of what I knew to be one of her signs. There is one on Cooper Street that I will see tomorrow.

Of course, I am looking at them in the way my sister would urge me. And yet I have not found the courage to see her.

Her fame brought the crowds to Hershey Street—there is no doubt about it. However, I don't think she's to blame. Or maybe it's that any feelings of anger I might have concerning the loss of our street are immediately quieted by the weight of her signs. When I see them, I believe that I am seeing more than most.

The feelings that anchored me the other day to the sign, *Slow to Bridge,* were not feelings as much as they were remembrances. I think I see our childhood in that sign.

Sometimes I stand there with four or five others. We look on in silence—each of us on individual paths, consulting the signs for direction. The others do not recognize me as the sister. I stand there, and am brought back to the highlights of my past. I can remember things in a way I cannot at the head of the "new" Hershey Street. I believe that if I saw my sister she would tell me more about my life, but if I have learned anything from my past, it's that I must pace myself.

I will never forget that day on the Deluxe QB train. We were on our way to Wyoming and feeling nervous about a young White man who stared out the window for the entire fifteen-hour ride. He answered all of our questions, but never turned his head from the window. When we reached Wyoming, he gathered his things and stumbled from the train. I watched him running toward the crowd of people awaiting arrivals. These people seemed eager for the train to move on, as they were probably disturbed by the congestion of life in such a small place. I watched as hard as I could as the man moved farther and farther out of my sight. His black coat flapped occasionally in the wind. He carried his suitcase slung across his back with his right arm, using the left arm to pump. This man was sprinting. Out of my sight. And just as he was about to disappear, he abruptly stopped. As though he had arrived home. But there was only dry brush around him. Then we were gone.

The train kept moving but I never forgot about the man. When I think of him, no matter where I am, my heart starts to race. I have never learned moderation in my thinking. I have damaged myself inexcusably.

At the corner of Fourth and Hershey, a few days ago, I made another attempt to reconcile the disappearance of my street and snuff out the probable ghosts. The new place is utterly foreign and has lost its charm as a "No Through Street." It's true. They opened it up. I stood at the corner and stared through the thoroughfare. Then I turned the corner and walked down four blocks to the other end of the "new" Hershey Street, observing the spot where I had just been standing. It was undeniable that a young man was now standing where I had been. He was looking down the corridor at me. Then a woman came and stood next to him, but perpendicularly, toward Fourth Avenue.

My eyes were glued to their performance, though my mind was elsewhere. Today I know for certain that my mind was nowhere near my sight, because for the life of me I cannot grasp what made me stand there. It is not as though I had achieved something and stood proud. Remember, I had walked around the block to reach the other end of Hershey Street, not conquered my anxiety by walking down it.

But it is the matter of my eyes stuck on that couple and their potential beauty, their performing belonging, that ultimately confounds me. These people were the new inhabitants of my subverted street. How did I bear to look at them, much less give my mind to them—or not give my mind, but allow it to take leave as I stood enthralled by them?

From the newspaper, two days ago, I read that the Modern Museum commissioned my sister, "our beloved directionalist," to paint a mural along the interior walls of the museum. And though the immensity of the project excited me (I certainly recognized this invitation as a major achievement in her life), the scope of the project did not make much sense. The paper said the mural would be a retrospective layering of all her past signs, with her most acclaimed sign, No Through Street, being the frontispiece. That what once had been "simply" directional finally would be brought into the art "establishment." They said that she would gain from this notoriety and that her name again would be on the tongue of every critic.

I went to the Modern to see if I could understand more.

I was aware of the possibility of an actual encounter between my sister and me, but I went anyway—suddenly prepared for everything. All past and all future, at once, and any other knowledge that might come up.

The Modern Museum is its own empire, but never has been referred to as confusing. It has many floors and stairs that go up and down. The bottom floor begins with the '50s and the top floor carries the most reputable of now.

It is a building so clear in its designations that people favoring obscurity won't venture in.

These were the thoughts I carried with me to the museum. And as I stepped in, they were the thoughts that stayed with me. I was right about everything, except one thing.

The woman in tattered, paint-splashed clothes with kinky black and tan hair outlining the beginning of what probably will be a spectacular piece of art was not my sister. She didn't even attempt to impersonate her when I walked up. She simply said that she had never heard of me.

And I believe her. But then, where is my sister? And if this woman is the directionalist whom everyone knows about, who is my sister?

The train ride from east to west is much smoother than the reverse, especially when the passenger has done something that she will always regret. For example, when she has given up the long-awaited homecoming.

On the train, the passenger returns to familiar seats. In each one, though this is not her intention, she resumes an instinctual posture. She slumps in the seat, turns her head toward the window, and blinks at the passing terrain.

The train moves smartly with so many destinations that it essentially has none. I am trying to be smart on this train and forget about having once lived through proximity.

First Sleep

A person walks out into the morning from a dream and connects the dream to things. She says, "This is the front of the house, the decision I have made; I live right next door to it."

Another catches sight of herself seated in the diner down the street and turns away.

In one memorable night there were fourteen sleeps, such longing for time, and three trips to the bathroom. There was a partial body.

The next morning, neighbors—still in their nightclothes—grabbed and patted each other in the street.

The old woman who lives in the large house on the corner was in the street.

And also, I was in the street.

Last night, one says, I thought I met my twin. I had been afraid to fall asleep when she came in—just to borrow something. Our interaction was quick. She wanted my lighter. I told her where it was. She asked, "Are you cold?" I said, "No." She said, "Good" and closed the door. I was on the eighth sleep.

The first sleep—where the eyes are involved—gives me time to look around, another says. I usually say that I am seeing myself when I am asleep, but don't really mean that. I mean that I am first sleeping.

Though the length and tone of this particular night's sleep resembled that of any night, it did not leave us unaffected.

We awoke that morning with an immediate recognition that Mrs. Gladman had gone.

—

The story of a person who is second sleeping is agreed upon by all:

There is a new climate outside, some showers. She wakes and goes for a drink of water, then sleeps for an hour.

Her lover draws nearer. The lover has to pee, gets up and stumbles down the hall.

The old woman wakes up and does not wear her slippers. She goes to the window, rocks in her chair five times.

Shirley gets up and breathes on the window.

———

Days ago there was a fire in the store, the green one on the corner, and a crowd outside.

Eleven days in the city, it is too hot to lie down. Women sweat and drink tea. My lover talks to her mom.

The neighborhood gets excited to put out a fire. Fires do not scare us.

After everybody swept sand into the fire, Señora Hernández had a barbecue. Soon there were rumors circulating about the new people:

The family next door owns a restaurant—not that anyone I know has ever been.

I could like their food, but not the fact that they own it. Anybody owning food has been understood.

Then they were saying the grandmother of that family took too much meat at the barbecue, which may have been true, but I could not give much thought to it. It was a beautiful night; I was in love.

People like me know our place after a fire; we have to eat and then quickly go to bed.

In my mind—all that temperature. I wanted to garner it.

The body lying on the floor was thought to be a half-pint body. Figures walking away. Sleep not the same.

Many people dream through their ninth sleep because they are thinking intensely of something. In the morning, their minds are at rest.

———

On the night of Mrs. Gladman's disappearance, the old woman on the corner pretended to be at rest. Neighbors walked by wanting to talk to her, but saw that she was asleep.

Because it was twilight they knocked on my door.

That night I was having rice for dinner. It was good, but needed something. I put on my sweatshirt and went out to get it. Then something strange happened. I turned the corner and forgot where I was going. When I came back I found a brief note attached to my door. I looked around but saw no one.

All the women whose names fall under "s" in the phone book sleep soundly.

Mrs. Gladman would say strange things at night. They stand up straight, she would say.

The note on my door was written by Mrs. Gladman. I think the note on my door was written by her. Later I would reword it in my sixth sleep.

My lover wakes up. She is in a heavy sweat—had had too much coffee at dinner. In her sixth sleep she is not sleepy. She is irritable. Turns her back to me, does not breathe, faces me, will not open her eyes. Turns her back again. Awake now, I sit up in bed and lean against the wall. I know that in my sixth sleep I am to rescue her.

The note eventually said everything about dreaming. After eighteen rewrites I mailed it to my friends thinking I had stumbled upon something.

―

When women walk down the street the old woman on the corner yells at them, and Señora Hernández yells at the old woman. Because she is yelling my downstairs neighbor begins to yell. Then a man comes running out of the corner store. He wants to be in the middle of something. He rushes out, finds nothing. I want to tell him that the people in this neighborhood do not yell in the street; they pick their teeth from the window.

Mrs. Gladman taught me to detail life completely. Now I can discern any situation and give assistance to the people in need.

The afternoon of the night of fourteen sleeps I was feeling the need to calculate. In one week I had had two long nights, a short morning, and a rainy one. I had walked down the street and become startled by a mural just painted there and upset that it was still wet. I had had no nocturnal episodes.

A person so tired that she cannot learn puts too much relish on things.

She imagines she has found Mrs. Gladman.

———

Something has settled in me when I am third sleeping. Almost on top of the lover. I am so tired. Almost the lover's body. I have to wake up and kiss her but I am too tired. This is really comfortable. The lover is away, but her body knows me. I want to kiss it. In my third sleep I am trying to mumble something about kissing. In this sleep I sound funny.

A sleep interrupted by ringing.

When the phone rang I ran out of the room to answer it. The point at which I returned marked the beginning of the partial body.

A person makes a chart in her room; the room bears a resemblance to the chart. Inside of the chart is the periphery of the person's body. She places the chart against the wall and stares at it. Half of the body falls.

I ran into the room and then quickly out of it, having realized I did not want to be there.

———

I wake my lover and answer many of her unasked questions when I am tenth sleeping. I tell her that I think she is dynamic and that I think I am in love with her. She is moved but really sleepy.

A mother thinks of her daughter in a quiet night—wants to write her a note. She sees herself in the daughter and feels good about it.

Once every two hundred and eighty sleeps the person's mind clears. The places of things make sense. She thinks, I am alive and so all these things.

But the search makes us tired.

When a neighborhood loses its center, there is no refuge. The people stay indoors, or if they have spent their lives indoors they begin to wander the street.

> On the street today this old woman leaning.
> A stout man walks by her. He looks at me.
> I think I know him from somewhere.
> Another man turns the corner.
> The old woman tries to trip him but is too slow.
> Then it turns out that they're together.
> He waits while she goes to the corner store.
>
> I decide to wait with him, but with my head down.

People who are outside with their heads down seem depressed about something.

Nice passersby would like to approach them.

Because there are so many people in a city with their heads down, nice people start to get mad.

A young girl walked by mad at me. She does not know Mrs. Gladman.

There are eleven of us on equidistant corners in this city who are sad and looking for her.

Mrs. Gladman is in us, but nowhere to be found.

Then we go home and sleep.

—

On every twenty-third night—those doors that dreamers open and close to something, people dying inside. Everybody wakes knowing nothing. I wake having learned a little more about my lover but not a thing about myself. In the morning she makes me coffee. We try to talk about it.

The one tells the other: I want to exchange what you know about me for what I have gained on you.

Everyone wants to ask each other what they have learned about Mrs. Gladman, but she is the only one that nobody knows.

Mrs. Gladman's disappearance followed a premonition, though I do not remember who felt it.

Everyone wants to say they have felt it.

In my sleep, some say, I have had the premonition, until the premonition becomes rumored and five days later insight.

Five days later. The phone rings. I think. It's nearing dawn.

———

Out of bed. There is minimal commotion. Down the street old people getting up.

In thirty-five years I will be getting up, but today.

Later, a person stands at her window wanting to know what's going on.

A child running by outside turns to me.

As after a major flood, the people returning home are thought "new" by the neighborhood. This morning I opened my shades thinking I'm not new as I watched Shirley pick her weeds.